A CHILDREN'S PROBLEM SOLVING BOOK

I'm Lost

Written by Elizabeth Crary   Illustrated by Marina Megale

Parenting Press, Inc.

SEATTLE, WASHINGTON

Parenting Press, Inc.
P.O. Box 75267
Seattle, Washington 98175
www.ParentingPress.com

Ways to teach children how to solve social problems are thoroughly explained in Problem-Solving Techniques in Childrearing *by Myrna B. Shure and George Spivack, San Francisco: Jossey-Bass Publishers, 1978.*

Text Copyright © 1985, 1996 by Elizabeth Crary
Illustrations Copyright © 1985, 1996 by Marina Megale
All rights reserved including the right of reproduction in whole or in part in any form.
First edition, 1985
Second edition, 1996
Printed in the United States of America

Book design by Elizabeth Watson
Formatting by Margarite D. Hargrave

Library of Congress Cataloging-in-Publication Data
Crary, Elizabeth, 1942-
        I'm lost / by Elizabeth Crary ; illustrated by Marina Megale. – 2nd ed.
            p.   cm. – (A children's problem solving book)
        Summary: Presents a situation where a child is lost at the zoo and encourages critical thinking on the part of the reader to resolve the problem.
        ISBN 1-884734-25-1 (library binding). – ISBN 1-884734-24-3 (paperback)
        1. Problem solving–Problems, exercises, etc.–Juvenile literature.   2. Missing children–Problems, exercises, etc.–Juvenile literature.   [1. Problem solving.   2. Lost children.]
        I. Megale, Marina, ill.   II. Title.   III. Series: Crary, Elizabeth, 1942-   Children's problem solving book.
        BF441.C7   1996
        153.4'3–dc20
                                                                                                    96-21283
                                                                                                         CIP

Parents (and Others) Can Teach Children How to Think

I wrote the six *Children's Problem Solving Books* to help children learn
to solve social problems. Each book explores a common problem for children:
sharing, waiting, wanting, being lost, and name calling. These books are interactive,
and children have fun thinking about the questions. Your young listener/reader will
enjoy helping the children in the stories decide what to do to solve their problems.

Why These Books Look Different

These books look different because they do something different. They teach children to think about the problems they face. These books help in three ways. First, they model a process for thinking before acting. Second, they offer children several different ways to handle each situation. Third, they show children how one person's behavior affects other people. Research shows that the more ideas a child has to solve social problems, the better his or her social adjustment is.

How to Use These Books

You will find questions to ask your child on almost every page. Before you read the *italic* words, give your child time to think about the question and answer it her- or himself. Each time a CHOICE (in the gray box) is offered, let her or him choose what to do. Turn to the page selected to see what happens. There are no "right" or "wrong" answers. All alternatives teach children to think. The outcomes of each allow children to discover for themselves why some actions are more effective than others.

I have included questions about feelings to encourage children to think about how they and others feel when there is a problem. Children need to know that feelings are not "good" or "bad," they just are. Awareness of feelings helps children think of solutions that meet their own and other's needs.

Transition from Story to Real Life

The last page of each book invites readers to list their own ideas about other ways to solve the story child's problem. With guidance your child can use the techniques learned in the book to think of ways to solve problems he or she has. For children who are reluctant to talk about solutions to their personal problems, you can ask them what the character in the book might do in a situation similar to theirs.

Through reading these books you are helping your child learn how to make good decisions. Further, you are teaching her or him that thinking and learning are fun. Children learn to think by thinking, not by being told what to do. Give your child many opportunities to practice thinking and problem solving. Have fun!

Elizabeth Crary
Seattle, Washington

This is a story about Gabriela.
Usually she has lots of fun.
She likes to play with toys, go to the zoo, and play ball at the park.

Today is a special day for Gabriela.

She and her dad are going on a trip to the zoo.

Gabriela likes to ride on her dad's lap, and then hop off to look at the
  animals up close.

But now Gabriela is unhappy.

Somehow she got separated from her dad.

She is lost.

What can Gabriela do to find her dad?

(Wait for child to respond after each question. Look at page 3, "How to Use These Books," for ways to encourage children to think for themselves.)

CHOICES

Gabriela can think of seven ideas. She can—

Stay where she is . . . . *page 10*

Go hunt for her dad. . . . . *page 14*

Cry. . . . . *page 16*

Look for a police officer . . . . *page 18*

Find a woman with small children . . . . *page 20*

Ask a clerk for help . . . . *page 22*

Wait at the front gate . . . . *page 26*

What will she try first?

(Wait for child to respond. Then turn to the appropriate page and continue the story.)

9

Stay where she is

Gabriela decides to stay where she is.

Her dad once said, "If you're lost stay where you are and I will find you."

She looks around for her dad.

Gabriela gets very tired of waiting.

How does Gabriela feel?

Anxious. She does not know where her dad is.

CHOICES

What do you think Gabriela will do next?

Continue to wait . . . . *page 12*

Go hunt for her dad. . . . . *page 14*

Continue to wait

Gabriela decides to wait longer.

She feels lonely sitting and waiting.

Finally her dad comes up. She runs to meet him.

He says, "I am so glad I found you, Gaby! I was so worried. Thank you for staying where you were."

How do you like this ending?

Let's pretend that Gabriela is tired of waiting and still has not found her dad.

CHOICES

What do you think Gabriela will do next?

Go hunt for her dad. . . . . *page 14*

Cry. . . . . *page 16*

Look for a police officer . . . . *page 18*

Go hunt for her dad

Gabriela decides to go look for her dad.
She walks along until the path divides.
Gabriela wonders which way her dad went.

How does Gabriela feel now?
Scared. She doesn't know which way her dad went.

CHOICES
What will Gabriela do now?
Cry . . . . *page 16*
Look for a police officer . . . . *page 18*

Cry

Gabriela decides to cry. She sits down and leans against a tree. She cries, and cries, and cries.

Finally she stops crying, but she is still lost.

She thinks about what she can do.

She remembers that her dad once said, "If you ever need help you can ask a police officer or a woman with small children or a store clerk."

How does Gabriela feel now?

Lonely and scared. She has not found her dad.

CHOICES

What do you think Gabriela will do next?

Look for a police officer . . . . *page 18*

Find a woman with small children . . . . *page 20*

Look for a police officer

Gabriela remembers that police help children when they are lost. Gabriela decides to stand on a picnic table and look for a police officer. She sees lots of people, but not her dad or a police officer.

How does Gabriela feel?
Worried. She is still lost.

CHOICES
What will Gabriela do next?

Find a woman with small children . . . . *page 20*
Ask a clerk for help . . . . *page 22*

Find a woman with small children

Gabriela sees a woman with a small child by the pony farm.

She runs to the woman and says, "Hello, my name is Gabriela. I lost my dad. Can you help me find him?"

"Yes, I can help you," the woman replies. "I will ask someone in the office to find your dad for you."

How does Gabriela feel now?

Happy and scared. Happy that the woman said she will help her find her dad. Scared that she might not be able to find him.

Will she find her dad?

(Turn to page 24.)

Ask a clerk for help

Gabriela decides to find a clerk. She remembers where a refreshment stand is and walks back to it.

Gabriela tells the cashier, "My name is Gabriela and I'm lost."

Then she asks, "Can you help me?"

"Yes, I can," says the woman. She phones the office to get help.

How does Gabriela feel?

Glad and sad. Glad that the woman can help. Sad because her dad is not found yet.

(Turn to page 24.)

A guard comes from the office.

The guard asks Gabriela her dad's name and what he looks like.

Gabriela says, "His name is Tom Chavez. He has dark hair and a wheelchair."

Gabriela and the guard walk back to the office near the front gate.

The guard uses the speaker to ask Tom Chavez to come to the office.

How does Gabriela feel now?

Glad. Glad that someone will help her find her dad.

(Turn to page 26.)

Wait at the front gate

Gabriela waits by the front gate. She remembers that her brother often waits for their dad at the front door of stores.

She hopes her dad will find her at the front gate.

While she waits for her dad, she talks to the guard.

How does Gabriela feel now?

Happy and worried. Happy because the guard called her dad on the loud speaker.

Worried that maybe he didn't hear it.

(Turn the page.)

Gabriela waits for a while. Then her dad comes.

When Gabriela sees her dad, she runs to meet him.

He hugs her and says, "I'm so glad I found you, Gaby. I was worried because I didn't know where you were."

Gabriela laughs, and says that she was worried, too.

How does Gabriela feel now?

Happy, happy, happy! Happy because she has found her dad.

How do you like this ending?

29

Idea page

Here is a list of Gabriela's ideas.

Start your own list of things you can do if you get lost. Add more ideas as you think of them. Ask your mom or dad what they want you to do if you get lost. Have fun!

Gabriela's ideas

✓ Stay where she is
✓ Go hunt for her dad
✓ Cry
✓ Look for a police officer
✓ Find a woman with children to help her
✓ Ask a clerk for help
✓ Wait at the front gate

Your ideas

Solving social problems…

Children's Problem Solving Books teach children to think about their problems. Each interactive story allows the reader to choose the main character's actions and see the result. Useful with 3–9-year-olds. Aligned with the K-3 Common Core State Standards (English Language: Reading/Literature). 32 pages, illustrated. $9.95 each, paperback. Written by Elizabeth Crary.

PROBLEM SOLVING

Megan and Amy want to play with the same truck.
ISBN 978-1884734-14-4

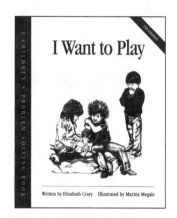

Danny is tired of playing alone and wants to share friends.
ISBN 978-1884734-18-2

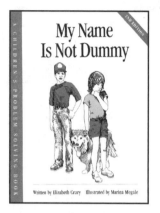

Jenny doesn't like being called "dummy."
ISBN 978-1-884734-16-8

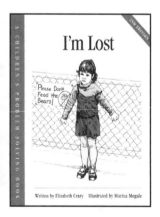

Gabriela is unhappy because she's lost her dad at the zoo.
ISBN 978-1884734-24-3

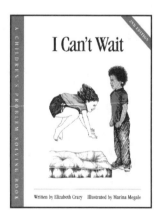

Luke wants his turn to jump on the mattress NOW!
ISBN 978-1-884734-22-9

Matthew doesn't want to stay with the babysitter.
ISBN 978-1-884734-20-5

Ask for these books at your favorite storefront or online bookstore, call Independent Publishers Group at 1-800-888-4741, or visit us on the Internet at www.ParentingPress.com.
Visa and MasterCard accepted. A complete catalog available online.

Parenting Press, Inc., P.O. Box 75267, Seattle, WA 98175

Prices subject to change without notice.

DEALING WITH FEELINGS

Coping with intense feelings…

Dealing with Feelings books acknowledge six intense feelings. Children discover safe and creative ways to express them. Each interactive story allows the reader to choose the main character's actions and see the result. Useful with ages 3-9 years. Aligned with the K-3 Common Core State Standards (English Language: Reading/Literature). 32 pages, illustrated. $9.95 each, paperback. Written by Elizabeth Crary.

ISBN 978-0-943990-62-0

ISBN 978-0-943990-64-4

ISBN 978-0-943990-66-8

ISBN 978-0-943990-93-4

ISBN 978-0-943990-89-7

ISBN 978-0-943990-91-0

Ask for these books at your favorite storefront or online bookstore, call Independent Publishers Group at 1-800-888-4741, or visit us on the Internet at www.ParentingPress.com. Visa and MasterCard accepted. A complete catalog available online.

Parenting Press, Inc., P.O. Box 75267, Seattle, WA 98175

Prices subject to change without notice.